# DEATH AT THE DOOR